# CHICAGO AND THE CAT

# The Camping Trip

*WRITTEN AND ILLUSTRATED BY*

# Robin Michal Koontz

PUFFIN BOOKS

For Alden Capen, who loved the woods

PUFFIN BOOKS
Published by the Penguin Group
Penguin Books USA Inc., 375 Hudson Street, New York, New York 10014, U.S.A.
Penguin Books Ltd, 27 Wrights Lane, London W8 5TZ, England
Penguin Books Australia Ltd, Ringwood, Victoria, Australia
Penguin Books Canada Ltd, 10 Alcorn Avenue, Toronto, Ontario, Canada M4V 3B2
Penguin Books (N.Z.) Ltd, 182-190 Wairau Road, Auckland 10, New Zealand

Penguin Books Ltd, Registered Offices: Harmondsworth, Middlesex, England

First published in the United States of America by Cobblehill Books,
an affiliate of Dutton Children's Books, a division of Penguin Books USA Inc., 1994
Published in a Puffin Easy-to-Read edition, 1997

1  3  5  7  9  10  8  6  4  2

Puffin® and Easy-to-Read® are registered trademarks of Penguin Books USA Inc.

THE LIBRARY OF CONGRESS HAS CATALOGED THE COBBLEHILL EDITION AS FOLLOWS:
Koontz, Robin Michal.
Chicago and the cat: the camping trip /
written and illustrated by Robin Michal Koontz.
p.  cm.
Summary: A rabbit and a cat go on a camping trip that includes hiking,
river rafting, and some surprises.
ISBN 0-525-65137-3
[1. Rabbits—Fiction. 2. Cats—Fiction. 3. Camping—Fiction.] I. Title.
PZ7.K83574Ci 1994 [E]—dc20 92-46685 CIP AC

Puffin Easy-to-Read ISBN 0-14-038603-3
Printed in the United States of America

Reading Level 2.1

# CHAPTER ONE

"Let's go camping this weekend!"
said Chicago.
"What for?" asked the cat.

"So we can pitch our tent
under the stars," said Chicago.
"And enjoy the beauty of the woods."

"We can pitch our tent
in the backyard," said the cat.
"And we can rent a movie
about the woods."

"I'll make my special
   campfire stew," said Chicago.
"Now you're talking," said the cat.
"Let's go camping!"

Chicago and the cat
headed for the campground.
"Isn't it beautiful
out here?" asked Chicago.
"Sure," said the cat.
"When do we eat?"

"If you put up the tent,

   I'll make the stew," said Chicago.

"Okay," said the cat.

"Yum, I can hardly wait

   for some of that stew!"

"Pee-yew!" cried the cat,

"what is that smell?"

"My stew is ready!" exclaimed Chicago.

"Nuts, berries, mushrooms, bark,

  you name it, it's in here!"

"Yuk!" cried the cat.

"Pass the tuna fish."

"I didn't pack any," said Chicago.

"Come on, try some of my stew."

"Forget it," said the cat.

She stomped off.

"You don't know what's good,"

Chicago mumbled.

She tasted the stew.

"*Eeee-yoww!*" cried Chicago.

She was burying the stew

when the cat came back.

"Where have you been?" asked Chicago.

"At the grocery store

down the road," replied the cat.

"Let's eat!" said Chicago.

# CHAPTER TWO

"Please pass the potato chips,"
   said the cat.
"You've had enough to eat," said Chicago.
"It's time to go to sleep."

"GURRR!"

"What was that?" cried the cat.

"It sounded like a bear," said Chicago.

"What will we do?" yelled the cat.

"No problem," said Chicago.

"Just look up 'bear' in my field guide."

Just then the bear appeared.

*"GROWWWLLL!"*

"Here, b-b-bear," said Chicago.

She tossed the bag of

potato chips at the bear.

"Hey, Chicago, it says here

not to feed it!" said the cat.

Chicago ran outside.

The bear ran after her.

"Hey, Chicago, it says here

not to run from it!" cried the cat.

Chicago climbed a tree.

"Hey, Chicago, it says here

bears climb trees!"

"GROOOOWWWWLLLLLL!"

cried the bear.

"*MEOW!*" yelled the cat.

The bear looked at the cat.

The cat flattened her ears

and extended her claws.

"*MEOWWW-ROWWWLLLL!*"

screamed the cat.

She raced toward the bear.

The bear ran into the woods.

"Wow, thanks," said Chicago.

"How did you do that?"

"No problem," said the cat.

"I looked up 'mountain lion'
in your field guide."

# CHAPTER THREE

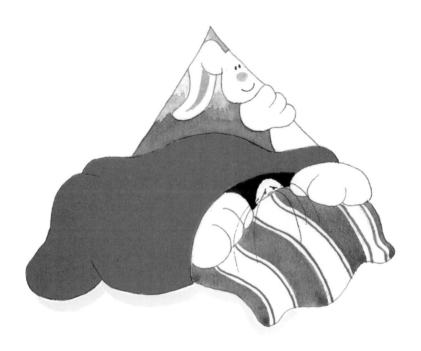

"Wake up!" yelled Chicago.

"I'm up already," said the cat.

"Who can sleep with
  all this noise?"

"Those are woodland sounds,"
   said Chicago.
"I didn't know trees
   were so noisy," said the cat.

"Stop complaining," said Chicago.
"Let's take a hike!"
"Can't we take a bus?" asked the cat.
"You lazy cat," said Chicago.
"Let's walk up the mountain."

"What for?" asked the cat.

"You can see all around
   from the top," replied Chicago.

"So what?" asked the cat.

"On the way we'll see
   lots of flowers and birds,"
   said Chicago.

"Birds?" said the cat.

"Let's take a hike!"

Chicago and the cat

started up the mountain.

"I don't see any birds,"

remarked the cat.

"Puff, puff, puff," replied Chicago.

"Are you all right?" asked the cat.

"Let me rest for a minute,"

said Chicago.

"How much farther?" she asked.

The cat looked up.

She looked down.

"That depends on which way
you're going," said the cat.

"Let's go the shortest way,"
suggested Chicago.

"Follow me," said the cat.

Soon they were back
at the campsite.
"Time for lunch!" said the cat.
"Then a nap?" asked Chicago.
"You bet," said the cat.

# CHAPTER FOUR

"Guess what we're doing next!"
 said Chicago.
"I give up," said the cat.
"River rafting!" said Chicago.

"Forget it," said the cat.

"You know I don't like water."

"I promise you won't get wet,"
  said Chicago.

"And we may see some fish."

"Fish?" exclaimed the cat.

"Let's go river rafting!"

Chicago and the cat headed
to the river.
They put on life vests
and got into the raft.
"Are you sure this is safe?"
asked the cat.
The guide pushed off
from the shore.

"Isn't this fun?" asked Chicago.

"No," replied the cat.

"I don't see any fish,
and my feet are wet."

"Sit back and enjoy the ride,"
said Chicago.

"Hang on!" yelled the guide.

"*AKKKKKKKKKKKK!*"
cried Chicago and the cat.

Finally the raft glided to a stop.

Chicago and the cat

slopped back to the campsite.

"River rafting was not
  what I expected," said Chicago.
"It was just what I
  expected," said the cat.
"Now, how about some
  real campfire stew?"
"What do you mean?" asked Chicago.
"From a can," replied the cat.
"Sounds great," said Chicago.
"Let's eat!"

# CHAPTER FIVE

"Guess what we're doing
tomorrow!" said Chicago.
"Isn't it my turn to decide
what we're doing?" asked the cat.

"Okay," said Chicago.

"So what are we doing tomorrow?"

"Nothing," said the cat.

She yawned and stretched.

"Nothing?" asked Chicago.

"That's right," said the cat.

Chicago looked up at the stars.
She listened to the
sound of the river.
"I like your idea," said Chicago.
"I knew you would," said the cat.
"Now, please pass the potato chips."